TEN DOGS IN THE WINDOW

A Countdown Book by Claire Masurel
Illustrated by Pamela Paparone

North-South Books · New York · London

Text copyright © 1997 by Claire Masurel. Illustrations copyright © 1997 by Pamela Paparone.
All rights reserved. No part of this book may be reproduced or utilized in any form or by any
means, electronic or mechanical, including photocopying, recording, or any information storage
and retrieval system, without permission in writing from the publisher. Published in the United
States by North-South Books Inc., New York. Published simultaneously in Great Britain, Canada,
Australia, and New Zealand in 1997 by North-South Books, an imprint of Nord-Süd Verlag AG,
Gossau Zürich, Switzerland. Library of Congress Cataloging-in-Publication Data is available.
A CIP catalogue record for this book is available from The British Library. For more information
about out books and the authors and artists who create them, visit our web site:
http://www.northsouth.com. The artwork was created with acrylic paint.
Designed by Marc Cheshire. Printed in Belgium
ISBN 1-55858-754-3 (trade binding) 10 9 8 7 6 5 4 3 2 1
ISBN 1-55858-755-1 (library binding) 10 9 8 7 6 5 4 3 2 1

For Meg—CM
For Sam Dylan Overmyer—PP

10 dogs in the window for the whole wide world to see.
Look, someone is coming. . . .

"You're the perfect dog for me!"

9 dogs in the window for the whole wide world to see.
Look, someone is coming. . . .

"You're the perfect dog for me!"

8 dogs in the window for the whole wide world to see.
Look, someone is coming. . . .

"You're the perfect dog for me!"

7 dogs in the window for the whole wide world to see.
Look, someone is coming. . . .

"You're the perfect dog for me!"

6 dogs in the window for the whole wide world to see.
Look, someone is coming. . . .

"You're the perfect dog for me!"

5 dogs in the window for the whole wide world to see.
Look, someone is coming. . . .

"You're the perfect dog for me!"

4 dogs in the window for the whole wide world to see.
Look, someone is coming. . . .

"You're the perfect dog for me!"

3 dogs in the window for the whole wide world to see.
Look, someone is coming. . . .

"You're the perfect dog for me!"

2 dogs in the window for the whole wide world to see.
Look, someone is coming. . . .

"You're the perfect dog for me!"

1 dog in the window. She's as lonely as can be.

Look, someone is coming. . . .

And here's his family!

1 dog in the window. She is making such a fuss. Look, they all are stopping. . . .

"You're the perfect dog for us!"